First Edition

HOOPOE

Published by Hoopoe Books,
a division of The Institute for the Study of Human Knowledge

ISBN 1-883536-19-7
Library of Congress Cataloging-in-Publication Data

Shah, Idries, 1924-
        The silly chicken / written by Idries Shah ; illustrated by Jeff Jackson.— 1st ed.
            p. cm.
        Summary: A Sufi teaching tale of a chicken that has learned to speak as people do and
                spreads an alarming warning, which causes the townspeople panic without first
                considering the messenger.
        ISBN 1-883536-19-7
        [1. Folklore.] I. Jackson, Jeff, 1971- ill. II. Title.

PZ8.S336 Si 2000
398.22--dc21
[E]
                                                                    99-051506

The Silly Chicken

Written by
Idries Shah

Illustrated by
Jeff Jackson

Once upon a time in a country far away, there was a town, and in the town there was a chicken, and he was a very silly chicken indeed. He went about saying "Tuck-tuck-tuck, tuck-tuck-tuck, tuck-tuck-tuck." And nobody knew what he meant.

Of course, he didn't mean anything at all, but nobody knew that. They thought that "Tuck-tuck-tuck, tuck-tuck-tuck, tuck-tuck-tuck" must mean something.

Now, a very clever man came to the town, and he decided to see if he could find out what the chicken meant by "Tuck-tuck-tuck, tuck-tuck-tuck, tuck-tuck-tuck."

First he tried to learn the chicken's language. He tried, and he tried, and he tried. But all he learned to say was "Tuck-tuck-tuck, tuck-tuck-tuck, tuck-tuck-tuck." Unfortunately, although he sounded just like the chicken, he had no idea what he was saying.

Then he decided to teach the chicken to speak our kind of language. He tried, and he tried, and he tried. It took him quite a long time, but in the end, the chicken could speak perfectly well, just like you and me.

After learning to speak as we do, the chicken went into the main street of the town and called out, "The earth is going to swallow us up!" At first the people didn't hear what he was saying because they didn't expect a chicken to be talking human language.

The chicken called out again, "The earth
is going to swallow us up!" This time the
people heard him, and they began to cry out,

"Good heavens!"

"Good gracious!"

"Dear me!"

"The earth is going
to swallow us up!"

"Yes, indeed! The
chicken says so!"

Thoroughly alarmed, all the people
packed up their most precious things and
began to run to get away from the earth.

They ran from one town ...

to another.

They ran through the fields ...

and into the woods and across the meadows.

They ran up the mountains ...

and down the mountains.

They ran down the world and up the world ...

and around the world.

They ran in every possible direction. But
they still couldn't get away from the earth.

Finally they came back to their town. And there was the chicken, just where they had left him before they started running.

"How do you know the earth is going to swallow us up?" they asked the chicken.

"I don't know," said the chicken.

At first the people were astonished, and they said again and again, "You don't know? You don't know? You don't know?"

And they became furious, and they glared sternly at the chicken and spoke in angry voices.

"How could you tell us such a thing?"

"How dare you!"

"You made us run from one town to another!"

"You made us run through the fields and into the
woods and across the meadows!"

"You made us run
down the world and
up the world and
around the world!"

"You made us run in every possible direction!"

"And all the while we thought you knew the earth was going to swallow us up!"

The chicken smoothed his feathers and cackled and said, "Well, that just shows how silly you are! Only silly people would listen to a chicken in the first place. You think a chicken knows something just because he can talk?"

At first the people just stared at the chicken, and then they began to laugh. They laughed, and they laughed, and they laughed because they realized how silly they had been, and they found that very funny indeed.

And the chicken would reply, "I am an egg."

The people would laugh at this, too, because
they knew he wasn't an egg, and they would say,
"If you're an egg, why aren't you yellow?"

"I am not yellow," the chicken would reply, "because I painted myself blue."

The people would laugh at this, too, because they could see he was not blue at all, and they would say, "What did you paint yourself with?"

And the chicken would reply, "With red ink."

And now people everywhere laugh at chickens and never take any notice of what they say — even if they can talk — because, of course, everybody knows that chickens are silly.

And that chicken still goes on and on in that town, in that far-away country, telling people things to make them laugh.

Other Books by Idries Shah

For Young Readers
The Clever Boy and the Terrible, Dangerous Animal
The Boy Without a Name
The Farmer's Wife
Neem the Half-Boy
The Lion Who Saw Himself in the Water
The Magic Horse
World Tales

Literature
The Hundred Tales of Wisdom
A Perfumed Scorpion
Caravan of Dreams
Wisdom of the Idiots
The Magic Monastery
The Dermis Probe

Novel
Kara Kush

Informal Beliefs
Oriental Magic
The Secret Lore of Magic

Humor
The Exploits of the Incomparable Mulla Nasrudin
The Pleasantries of the Incredible Mulla Nasrudin
The Subtleties of the Inimitable Mulla Nasrudin
Special Illumination

Travel
Destination Mecca

Human Thought
Learning How to Learn
The Elephant in the Dark
Thinkers of the East
Reflections
A Veiled Gazelle
Seeker After Truth

Sufi Studies
The Sufis
The Way of the Sufi
Tales of the Dervishes
The Book of the Book
Neglected Aspects of Sufi Study
The Commanding Self
Knowing How to Know

Studies of the English
Darkest England
The Natives are Restless